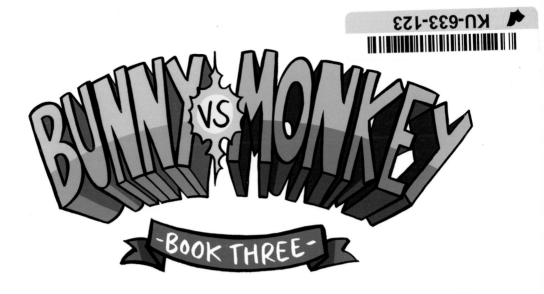

BUNNY vs MONKEY

-BOOK THREE-

YEAR TWO
JANUARY - JUNE

BY JAMIE SMART

Dedicated to the Phoenix editors
– Ben, Will and Tom,
and all the amazing crew
at The Phoenix and DFB!

Bunny vs Monkey: Book Three
is A DAVID FICKLING BOOK

First published in Great Britain in 2016 by
David Fickling Books,
31 Beaumont Street,
Oxford, OX1 2NP

978-1-910200-84-1
All rights reserved.

3 5 7 9 10 8 6 4

David Fickling Books reg. no. 8340307

A CIP catalogue record
for this book is available
from the British Library.

Printed and bound in Great Britain by Sterling.

Papers used by David Fickling Books are from
well-managed forests and other responsible sources.

CONTENTS!

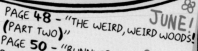

LIONEL

TUM TE
TUM
TE
TUM!

WHERE ARE YOU OFF TO WITH MY LEFT-OVER MINCE PIES, PIG?

THEY'RE FOR MY IMAGINARY FRIEND, LIONEL!

EVERY DAY, I LEAVE MINCE PIES IN THE SAME SPOT, THEN WHEN I COME BACK HE'S EATEN THEM!

WE'RE THE BEST OF FRIENDS!

WHAT'S PIG DOING OUT HERE?

HE SAYS HE HAS AN IMAGINARY FRIEND!

HERE YOU GO, LIONEL. ENJOY!

UMM, PIG? YOU DO KNOW THOSE MINCE PIES ARE JUST GOING TO BE EATEN BY OTHER ANIMALS?

HA HA, NOT IF LIONEL GETS THERE FIRST!

HALF AN HOUR LATER...

THERE, YOU SEE? LIONEL ATE THEM ALL! HEE HEE, SAME TIME TOMORROW, LIONEL!

NEXT DAY...

HEY, PIG! WE HEAR YOU HAVE AN IMAGINARY FRIEND!

LIONEL, YES.

HA HA. LIONEL.

8

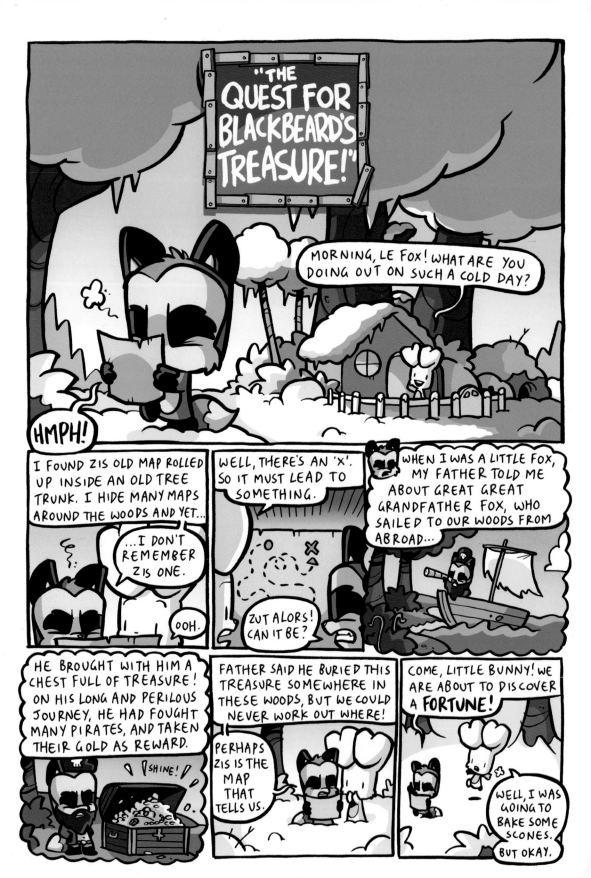

THERE YOU GO, FLOPSY. EAT UP, THERE'S PLENTY MORE WHERE THAT CAME FROM.

MIP!

SKUNKY! IS THAT THE WEIRD CREATURE YOU FOUND AT THE CENTRE OF THE EARTH?

EEK! INTRUDER!

OH, IT'S JUST BUNNY.

WHAT DO YOU MEAN 'JUST' BUNNY? ANYWAY, I DIDN'T INTRUDE, I FELL IN.

UH-OH. THE SNOZZIG-ATATRON MUST HAVE WEAKENED YOUR HOUSE FOUNDATIONS. I SHOULDN'T HAVE SET IT TO MAXIMUM OVERDRIVE.

IT'S JUST FLOPSY, YOU SEE. TURNS OUT HE HAS A FEROCIOUS APPETITE FOR SAUSAGES, AND THE ONLY WAY I COULD KEEP HIM FED WAS TO INVENT A DEVICE TO PRODUCE SAUSAGES AT HIGH SPEED!

CHUNK CHUNK CHUNK

GRAVEL

GRISTLE

GRIT

CHUNK CHUNK CHUNK

THUS, THE SNOZZIGATATRON!!

THAT'S WHAT'S BEEN MAKING ALL THE NOISE BENEATH MY FLOOR!

MY LAIR REACHES FAR AND WIDE UNDER THESE WOODS. IT'S NOT MY FAULT IF YOU LIVE ON TOP OF IT.

NOT YOUR FAULT? SKUNKY, EVERYTHING BAD THAT HAPPENS HERE IS YOUR FAULT.

NOW, HOW DO I TURN THIS THING OFF?

NOOOO!

CHUNK CHUNK!

IF YOU DEPRIVE FLOPSY OF HIS SAUSAGES, THERE'S NO TELLING WHAT HE'LL DO!

EAT SOMETHING ELSE, PROBABLY.

WELL, PROBABLY. BUT IS IT WORTH THE RISK?

THIS THING IS NOISY AND I WANT IT OFF!

NO! SAUSAGES!

THAT'S NOT AN ARGUMENT!

SAUSAGES!

MIP! MIP!

CHUNK!

#☆◎★⚡‼

CHUN HUNK! KRA CHU

CHUNK!

...BUNNY.

SNAP!

EEEEEEEE ÷ UH?

CHOMP! CHOMP! CHOMP!

FLOPSY? YOU... ...INFLATED?

WOW. HE SURE DOES LIKE SAUSAGES.

DOOMF!

MIP! NOM! MIP!

BUT I DIDN'T KNOW HE DID THAT.

THPTHBTH!

HEE HEE! IT SOUNDS LIKE YOU FARTED!

RUN, SKUNKY! FROM WHATEVER IS UNDERNEATH YOUR FLOOR!

OH.

OH YES.

SCARPER!

I AM NEVER, EVER, GOING BACK THERE AGAIN.

SNAKE!

BANG! BANG! BANG!

ONE DAY FLOPSY, LET'S GO DOWN THERE AGAIN.

MIP!

NEXT TIME - "CASA DEL PIG!"

"CASA DEL PIG!"

PIG? IT'S CHUCKING IT DOWN OUT HERE, WHY AREN'T YOU AT HOME?

I AM!

THIS UMBRELLA IS MY HOME! WHATEVER THE WEATHER, IT KEEPS ME SAFE.

ALL THIS TIME... YOU'VE BEEN LIVING UNDER AN UMBRELLA?

THIS WON'T DO, PIG. YOU NEED A HOUSE! SOMEWHERE TO LIVE!

WHERE DO PIGS LIVE?

UM...

I DON'T KNOW! HOORAY! BUT I WILL **BUILD MYSELF A HOUSE,** JUST LIKE THE REST OF YOU!

YAY!

FOOMPHH!

ONE RUSHED CONSTRUCTION LATER...

TAA DAA! A HOUSE IN THE TREES, JUST LIKE WEENIE!

I'VE ALWAYS WANTED A NEIGHBOUR!

URF...HUFF...OH, I FORGOT PIGS AREN'T VERY GOOD AT CLIMBING.

I CAN'T GET IN MY HOUSE!

SIGHH.

I COULD LIVE UNDERGROUND INSTEAD, JUST LIKE LE FOX!

I DON'T REMEMBER AGREEING TO ZIS.

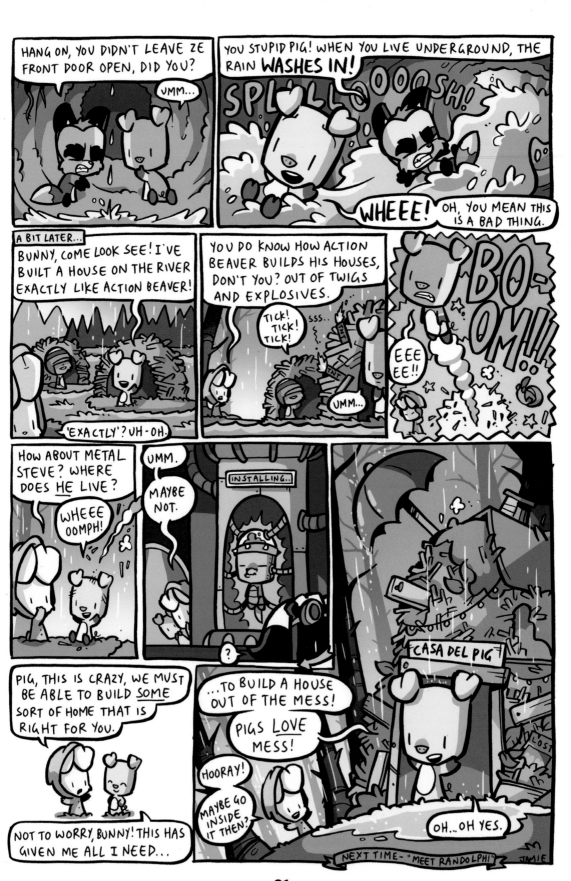

23

MARCH

"THE STENCH!"

MINE'S BIGGER!

NO! MINE IS!

HEY, WHAT ARE YOU TWO DOING? CAN I JOIN IN?

I'VE DECIDED TO RENOUNCE EVIL!!

I'M TIRED OF THAT SHRIEKING MONKEY TELLING ME TO SHUT UP. SO THIS MORNING, I WOKE UP AND I THOUGHT 'HEY! I WANT TO BE GOOD FROM NOW ON!'

THAT'S WONDERFUL, MISTER SKUNKY! YOU CAN JUDGE OUR 'TALLEST SUNFLOWER' CONTEST!

WE'VE BEEN GROWING THEM FOR MONTHS! PROTECTING THEM FROM WINTER!

THEY'RE SO SPECIAL!

HMM, WELL, I'D SAY...

WILT!!

...OH NO!

WILT!!

THEY DIED-ED! WHY DID THEY DIE?

POO! I THINK IT WAS SKUNKY'S SMELL! HE STINKS!

BUT I'M A SKUNK! I'M SUPPOSED TO SMELL!

STINKY STINK!

IT'S BURNING MY EYES!

BOO HOO! WHY MUST HE DESTROY EVERYTHING BEAUTIFUL?

I'M BEING SICK IN MY MOUTH!

GRR!

CONGRATULATIONS, METAL STEVE, YOU HAVE LEARNED HOW TO WRITE! NOW GO AND DISCOVER THE JOYS OF EXPRESSING YOURSELF IN A LETTER!

SCRIBBLE! SCRIBBLE! SCRIBBLE!

A FEW DAYS LATER...

MORNING, YOUNG LADY. IS THIS YOURS?

A REPLY!

FLUFFY ANIMALS!

BZZT! BZZT! DESTROY! BZZT!

NEXT TIME - "FISHY PLOPS!"

27

"FISHY PLOPS!"

WHAT... IS IT?

IS IT A FISH?

NO, OF COURSE IT'S A FISH, WEENIE. I JUST MEANT WHAT IS IT DOING HERE, IN THE MIDDLE OF THE WOODS?

AND WHY IS IT SO BIG?

FRRPP!

HEE HEE, IT'S ALL SQUISHY!

NICE TO CUDDLE!

FISH CUDDLES!

SORRY, BUT WE HAVE TO PUT IT BACK.

BACK WHERE?

IN THE RIVER. IT'S A FISH, IT BELONGS IN WATER.

MORNING!

SKUNKY! MONKEY! I SHOULD HAVE KNOWN THIS HAS SOMETHING TO DO WITH YOU.

WELL, WHATEVER IT IS, WE'RE DRAGGING IT BACK TO THE RIVER.

OH, THAT'S JUST FISHY PLOPS. A GIANT METAL FISH I CREATED, WRAPPED IN SYNTHETIC SKIN.

WHAT... WHAT DOES IT DO?

NOTHING.

NOTHING?

LITERALLY, NOTHING.

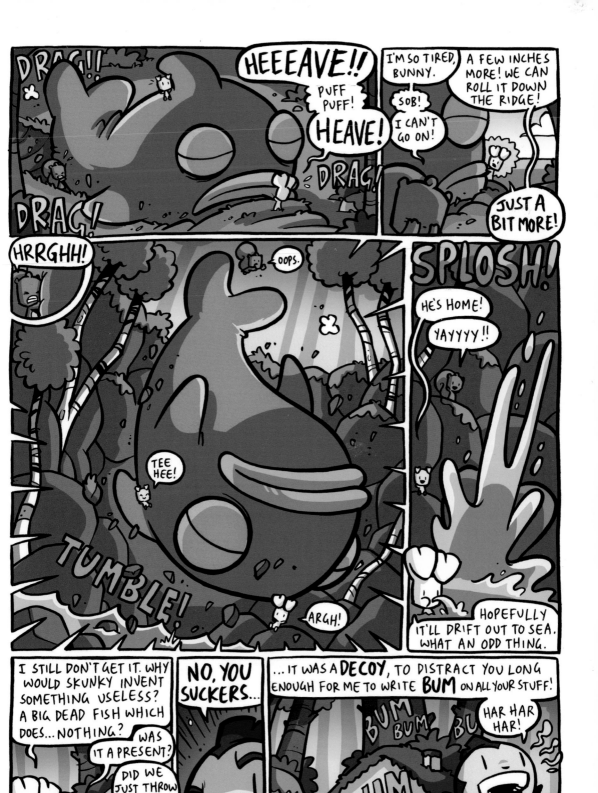

"THE BIGGEST, MOSTEST ENORMOUSEST EXPLOSION IN THE WORLD!"

DEEP IN SKUNKY'S LAIR...

I HAVE DONE IT! WITH THE WONDERS OF **SCIENCE**, I HAVE SYNTHESISED A MINUTE AMOUNT OF **BOOMANTIUM**, THE MOST VOLATILE SUBSTANCE EVER DISCOVERED, AND PUT IT INSIDE THIS **CARROT**.

A CARROT WHICH WOULD NOW CAUSE...

...THE BIGGEST, MOSTEST **ENORMOUSEST** EXPLOSION IN THE WORLD!!

WOOF!

NO, ACTION BEAVER. KEEP AWAY! THIS IS MY SECRET WEAPON, SHOULD MONKEY EVER GET OUT OF CONTROL, THE THREAT OF THIS **CARROT** WILL KEEP HIM IN LINE.

SUCH A POWERFUL VEGETABLE MUST BE KEPT LOCKED AWAY, SAFE AND UNDISTURBED.

COSY!

AHH, WHO'M I KIDDING? I WANT TO SHOW OFF HOW **BRILLIANT** I AM.

ABOVE GROUND...

LOOK, EVERYONE! THIS CARROT WOULD CAUSE THE BIGGEST, MOSTEST **ENORMOUSEST** EXPLOSION IN THE WORLD!

AND I MADE IT WITH **SCIENCE!**

APRIL

"BILLION-DOLLAR BEAVER!"

BZZZZZZZZZZZZZZZ

ALL I CAN SMELL IS BURNING FUR!

WE'RE NOT DOING THIS FOR FUN, MONKEY. WE'RE TESTING ACTION BEAVER'S RESISTANCE TO THE BIGGEST LASER IN MY LABORATORY!

PING PING!

NOPE, NOT EVEN A SCRATCH. I DON'T UNDERSTAND IT, HE'S INDESTRUCTABLE.

CLANG!!!

FRRP!

MONKEY!

YOU HAVE YOUR TESTS, I HAVE MINE.

ACTION BEAVER, STEP BEHIND MY MOLECULAR DNA ANALYSER. IT'LL GIVE US SOME CLUES.

GASP!

BOOP! BOOP!

WARNING!

CHEMICAL X DETECTED IN YOUR BLOODSTREAM!

IT'S THE MOST POWERFUL CHEMICAL EVER SYNTHESISED, AND SOMEHOW IT MUST HAVE GOT INSIDE HIM.

THPTH

I HAVE ACCIDENTALLY CREATED A SUPER BEAVER!

NOW, WHAT WOULD BE THE MOST RESPONSIBLE SCIENTIFIC USE OF SUCH A THING?

LEFT, BRIGSTOCKE! FOLLOW THE SCENT OF BURNING WOODLANDS!

SNIFF! SNIFF!

RANGER

DO YOU THINK THIS WAS WHERE THE EXPLOSION HAPPENED, SIR?

AT A GUESS.

GASP! LOOK AT IT, WHAT COULD HAVE POSSIBLY CAUSED SUCH DESTRUCTION?

DARNED KAKAPO.

I SEE YOU, UP THERE, CAUSING ALL THIS TROUBLE.

THE BIRDS, SIR?

NO, BRIGSTOCKE, THEIR POO! DARNED BIRDS EAT FERMENTED BERRIES, DO POOS FILLED WITH ETHANOL AND METHANE, THEN ONE SPARK AND...

KA-BOOM!

I'VE SEEN IT HAPPEN BEFORE.

EXPLOSIVE POO? THIS IS THE GREATEST DAY OF MY LIFE!

KING KAKAPO? HELLO?

IF THIS IS ABOUT THE POO, WE'RE NOT GOING TO STOP POOING.

I KNOW, BUT MAYBE STOP IT PILING UP?

IT HAS A TENDENCY TO BLOW UP. AND THAT ATTRACTS HUMANS.

FRRP!

WHO CARES? THIS IS GREAT!

IT WON'T BE SO GREAT WHEN THE HUMANS DISCOVER US. AND BY 'US', I MEAN YOU. AND BY 'YOU', I MEAN YOUR INVENTIONS.

NOT MY INVENTIONS! WHAT CAN WE DOOOO?

WE CAN WAIT UNTIL THE HUMANS GO, THEN YOU CAN HELP ME FIX IT.

A FEW WEEKS LATER...

WHAT.

THE.

A FULLY PLUMBED TOILET FOR BIRDS IS HARDLY MY GREATEST SCIENTIFIC ACHIEVEMENT.

I THINK IT'S PRETTY COOL, SKUNKY.

NEXT TIME - "MONKEY BUTLER!"

37

"MONKEY BUTLER!"

MEH HEH HEH!

HEH HEH.

HEH.

I DON'T NEED SKUNKY, I HAVE CREATED THE MOST INGENIOUS TRAP OF ALL!

A BAG FULL OF **FISH GUTS**, HANGING FROM A TREE!

PROUD!

AND UNDERNEATH, A **CARROT**. PERFECT BAIT FOR A BUNNY.

PLONK!

MISTER MONKEY! WHAT ARE YOU DOING?

I, UM...

WAIT...

WHAT ARE YOU DOING?

I AM LORD PIG PIGGINGTON OF PIGGYSHIRE!

AND I AM LADY WEENIE WHUFFINGTON WEENIE-ON-THE-WUFF.

WE ARE PLAYING POSH!

LOOK, I CAN'T HAVE YOU TWO SPOILING MY INGENIOUS TRAP. I NEED YOU TO NOT TELL ANYONE ABOUT THIS, OKAY?

HMM, WHAT IS IT WORTH, PEASANT?

SIGHHHH...

...ANYTHING. I'LL DO ANYTHING.

TEE HEE! THEN WE HAVE A SPLENDID IDEA!

TING-A-LING-A-LING-A-LING!

I SAY? I SAY?

GRRR! WHAT IS IT, YOUR LORDSHIP?

I ASKED YOU TO BRING ME TOAST OVER HALF AN HOUR AGO, MONKEY BUTLER!

YEAH, WELL, YOU ONLY GAVE ME A TABLE LAMP TO HEAT THE BREAD WITH... OW!

BOP!

DON'T TALK BACK, MONKEY BUTLER! KNOW YOUR PLACE!

GASP! FISH GUTS!

PLOOMP!

HAR HAR! SO LONG, POSHOS! I QUIT! THIS MONKEY IS NO ONE'S BUTLER!

BUNNY? YOU'RE NOT COVERED IN FISH GUTS!

I SHOULD HOPE NOT.

B... BUT... THE CARROT!

I THOUGHT THAT MIGHT BE A TRAP. LUCKILY, I DON'T EVEN LIKE CARROTS.

I PREFER PIE.

BUT IF YOU DIDN'T SPRING THE TRAP, THEN WHO...?

I DON'T BELIEVE IT, THE ONE DAY I DECIDE TO EAT HEALTHILY, AND I GET THIS!

GASP!

IS THIS YOUR DOING, MONKEY? THAT'S IT, I'M NEVER HELPING YOU EVER AGAIN!

NO! ARGH! I'M SORRY, SKUNKY! MY INVENTIONS ARE STUPID! DON'T LEAVE ME! DON'T LEEEEEEEEEAVE ME!

WELL, THERE IS ONE THING YOU COULD DO...

HAT BACK ON.

COME, MONKEY BUTLER! COME AND HELP ME SCRUB FISH GUTS OUT OF MY FUR!

EUGHH.

JAMIE

NEXT TIME - "THE BIG EYE AM!"

"THE PURPLE!"

IT'S... BEAUTIFUL!

THE **SATURN PURPLE**, ONE OF THE RAREST FLOWERS IN THESE WOODS. THEY SAY WHEN IT BLOOMS, YOU CAN HEAR ANGELS SINGING!

HMPH!

WELL, I THINK IT'S DISGUSTING. LOOK AT IT, ALL PRETTY AND COLOURFUL. UGH!

WHEN I OWN THE WOODS, I WILL BAN ALL NICE COLOURS.

THE BEST THING ABOUT THE SATURN BURPLE IS THAT YOU CAN PICK ITS SEEDS OFF...

...AND THEY SPLAT!

EEEEEEE!

LIKE BURPLE PAINT!

TWANG!

SPLAT!

PURPLE.

GET AWAY FROM ME! I WILL NOT BE TAINTED WITH THIS RANCID... **PURPLE!**

BURPLE!

NO. PURPLE.

C'MON MONKEY, IT'S FUN! IT'S LIKE PLAYING PAINTBALL!

SPLAT!

NO! NOOO!! ARGHHH!

NEXT TIME: "THE WEIRD, WEIRD WOODS!"

"THE WEIRD, WEIRD WOODS!"
-PART ONE-

ON THE EDGE OF THE WOODS THERE IS A MYSTERIOUS CABIN...

MYSTERIOUS, BECAUSE IT HOLDS ALL THE WOODS' MYSTERIES.

TINK A TINK A TINK

WORLD'S #1 RANGER

NOW. WHERE WERE WE?

THE WEIRD WOODS WALL

AND ONE MAN IS DETERMINED TO FIGURE THEM OUT.

PHEW! SURE IS DARK OUT THERE, FELT LIKE SOMETHING WAS WATCHING ME, TOO.

PROBABLY WAS!

YOU'RE NOT LOOKING AT YOUR WEIRD WOODS WALL AGAIN, ARE YOU? LET IT GO.

BUT THERE ARE TOO MANY STRANGE THINGS GOING ON!

MASSIVE EXPLOSIONS! CLANKING MACHINERY! DISTANT GIGGLING, MANIACAL LAUGHING AND GIRLY SCREAMING!

NOT TO MENTION THE THINGS WE'VE FOUND.

46

THAT GIANT EYEBALL EMBEDDED IN THE MIDDLE OF THE ROAD!

THE WEIRD, SPIKY, SKIN THAT BLEW INTO TOWN.

OR HOW ABOUT **THE HEAD OF AN ENORMOUS CHICKEN-SHAPED ZEPPELIN?!**

CLUCK!

SOMETHING'S GOING ON!

CALM DOWN, BRIGSTOCKE. MAYBE SOME THINGS ARE BETTER LEFT ALONE.

YOU! YOU KNOW WHAT'S GOING ON, DON'T YOU!

TELL ME W...

CREEEEAKK!

DID YOU HEAR SOMETHING?

YOU LEFT THE DOOR OPEN!

IT'S COMING INSIDE!

HOLD ME!

HOLD ME!

CREAKK!

WE'RE ATTACKING YOUR FORT! **BLOO BLOO BLOO BLOO!!**

BLOO.

SCREAM! SCREAM!

PERHAPS SOME MYSTERIES WILL NEVER BE ANSWERED...

WHY WAS THAT PIG DRESSED LIKE THAT?

OR MAYBE THEY WILL, IN PART TWO NEXT TIME!!

JUNE

"THE WEIRD, WEIRD WOODS!"
- PART TWO -

IT'S THE MIDDLE OF THE NIGHT, AND CRASHING THROUGH THE WOODS COME WEENIE AND PIG, PURSUED BY...

HUUUUMANS!

BLOO BLOO BLOO!

AH'M **BUNNY THE KID,** AND YOU, CHIEF RUNNING PIG, ARE ABOUT TO GET A TASTE OF WILD WEST JUSTICE!

POK!

YEEE-HAW!

THEY'RE... FIRING AT US!

SHRIEK!

I THOUGHT WE WERE JUST PLAYING!

WE WERE...

BUT THEN HUMANS STARTED CHASING US!

THE HUMANS? COMING INTO OUR WOODS?

ZUT ALORS! ZE PROPHECY IS FINALLY COMING TRUE!

I MUST DESTROY MY NETWORK OF TUNNELS, ELSE THEY GET HOLD OF MY SECRETS!

PUFF PUFF! I CAN'T KEEP UP, BRIGSTOCKE! YOU... YOU GO ON WITHOUT ME!

I WILL! THIS MAY BE OUR BEST CHANCE TO DISCOVER WHAT GOES ON IN THESE WOODS!

ACTION BEAVER! THIS IS THE MISSION YOU'VE BEEN TRAINING FOR!

ARE YOU READY?

SCHHHP!

I'D CALL THAT A 'YES'.

BOOM!

GO, ACTION BEAVER! DEFEND OUR WOODS FROM THE INVADERS!

CLONK!

ARGH!

I AM DESTROYING IT ALL, HUMAN!

BOOM!

?!

BOOM!

BOOM!

WHAT...

...WHAT'S GOING ON?

CRAWL!

HAR HAR! EVERYONE SEEMS TO BE OUT, SO I HALF-INCHED ALL OF WEENIE'S FRESHLY BAKED BUNS!

CHOMP!

RUSTLE!

PLEASE DON'T TAKE MY BUNS!

THIS PLACE IS INSANE! I CAN'T TAKE IT!

SCREAM!

SCREAM!

THAT WAS THE HUMAN INVASION? I BLEW EVERYTHING UP FOR NOTHING.

JAMIE

NEXT TIME : 'BUNNYOPIA!'

"BUNNY-OPIA!"

WELL HELLO THERE, BUNNY! COME ON IN TO **BUNNYOPIA!**

Welcome to BUNNY-OPIA!

RUB! RUB!

RUB! RUB!

WHAT'S WRONG? WE BEEN WAITIN' FOR YOU!

I THOUGHT THIS MIGHT BE A CHEESE DREAM.

I'VE NOT REALLY MET MANY OTHER BUNNIES BEFORE. I HAD NO IDEA THIS WAS HERE.

I JUST HAD THIS MYSTERIOUS INVITATION PUSHED UNDER MY DOOR AND, WELL, HERE YOU ALL ARE!

SHOOF!

WOULD YOU LIKE SOME **CARROT?**

I DON'T REALLY LIKE CARROTS.

YOU **LOVE** CARROTS. YOU JUST FORGOT.

HEE HEE.

NO REALLY, I...HANG ON, WHY DO YOU HAVE A **KEY** IN YOUR BACK?

WHY DO YOU **ALL** HAVE KEYS IN YOUR BACKS?

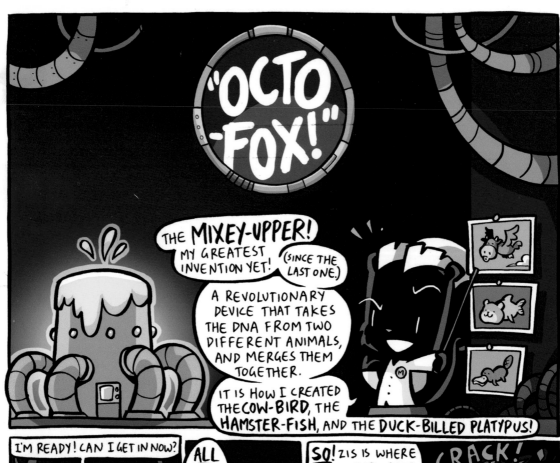

"OCTO-FOX!"

The **MIXEY-UPPER!** MY GREATEST INVENTION YET! (SINCE THE LAST ONE.)

A REVOLUTIONARY DEVICE THAT TAKES THE DNA FROM TWO DIFFERENT ANIMALS, AND MERGES THEM TOGETHER.

IT IS HOW I CREATED THE **COW-BIRD**, THE **HAMSTER-FISH**, AND THE **DUCK-BILLED PLATYPUS!**

I'M READY! CAN I GET IN NOW?

HOLD ON, MONKEY! FIRST WE HAVE TO PROGRAMME WHICH ANIMAL WE MIX YOU WITH!

ALL OF THEM!

SKK!

UH?

SO! ZIS IS WHERE YOU DESPICABLE FIENDS HIDE OUT, RIGHT BENEATH MY TUNNELS!

CRACK!

LE FOX!

HANG ON, WHAT'S...

SPLOSH!

EUGH!

NO! GET OUT OF THE MIXEY-UPPER!

FZZT! BANG!

ARGH! HE'S SHORT-CIRCUITED THE CONTROLS!

HE COULD BE MIXING WITH **ANYTHING.**

BLOOP! GLOOP!

"WEENIE'S BIG ADVENTURE!"

MISTER BEAR!

MISTER BEAR, WAKE UP!

YOU'VE OVERSLEPT, SILLY!

IT'S SUMMER ALREADY, AND YOU WERE SUPPOSED TO GET UP IN SPRING.

GRRWLL.

GRAFCKLYYG!!

SNIFF!

SNIFF SNIFF!

HEE HEE! I KNEW YOU'D APPRECIATE A CUPCAKE BREAKFAST!

I CAME TO ASK IF YOU'D LIKE TO JOIN ME ON A BIG ADVENTURE! EVERYONE ELSE IN THE WOODS IS BUSY, FIGHTING WITH EACH OTHER, BUT IT'S TOO BEAUTIFUL A DAY TO WASTE!

I HAVE A BACKPACK FULL OF FOOD AND NO PLAN!

WHAT DO YOU SAY?

YAYYYYYY!

I THINK WE'VE DONE EVERYTHING THERE IS TO DO ON EARTH TODAY, MISTER BEAR!

BUT THERE'S ONE PLACE LEFT WE HAVEN'T BEEN!

WHEEEEEHEEEE!!

PLUH!

HERE I COME, THE MOON!

CLONK!

OW! HEE HEE!

FELL A BIT SHORT.

LET'S GO AGAIN!

OKAY, THIS TIME, WE NEED MORE UP.

WEENIE?

WEENIE'S BEING EATEN BY THE BEAR!!

UH OH.

RUN, MISTER BEAR! WE'RE IN TROUBLE NOW!

GET AWAY FROM HIM!

RRF! RRF!

SOMETIME LATER...

IT'S BEEN A WHILE SINCE BUNNY STOPPED SEARCHING FOR US, AND I'M GETTING TIRED.

MAYBE WE SHOULD GO TO SLEEP NOW.

BECAUSE SOME DAYS ARE WORTH DREAMING ABOUT...

...ALL OVER AGAIN.

JAMIE

NEXT TIME: "BRAIN-ACHE!"

"BRAIN-ACHE!"

LOOK AT LE FOX. STANDING THERE, KNOWING LOADS. HE THINKS HE'S SO CLEVER!

HE _IS_. AND THAT'S WHY I CAREFULLY PUT THAT HELMET ON HIM!

WHAT? WHY?

BECAUSE IT IS ATTACHED TO THIS HELMET! LE FOX KNOWS MORE ABOUT THE WOODS THAN ANYONE, SO I THOUGHT WHAT IF WE COULD STEAL HIS BRAIN...

...AND PUT IT INTO YOU?

I HAVE INVENTED **BRAIN-SWAP** TECHNOLOGY!

EEE, PUT IT ON! PUT IT ON!

YOU BRUTISH OAFS, WHY HAVE YOU PUT THIS THING ON MY HEAD?

SHOVE!

ERK!

SILLY MISTER CATERPILLAR, YOU'D LOOK MUCH NICER IN BLUE.

PLONK!

OH! IS IT HAT DAY ALREADY?

ZZNAP

UH OH.

56

WHAT ARE YOU ALL DOING OUT HERE? THE BIG GRIZZLY BEAR IS GOING BACK INTO HIBERNATION TODAY, WE'LL ALL NEED TO STAY OUT OF HIS WAY.

HE'S **GRUMPY!**

HEY, WASN'T LE FOX AROUND HERE SOMEWHERE?

UMM.

I THINK LE FOX...

...MIGHT BE PIG NOW.

WHEE EEEE EEEE EEEE EEE!!

THAT'S FUNNY. I DON'T REMEMBER HAVING A BIG TAIL.

OR FUR.

OR A FRENCH ACCENT.

OR STANDING NEXT TO A BEAR.

GRRRWLL!

POKE!

POKE!

SHRIIIIEK! THERE'S A BIG BEAR CHASING ME FOR NO REASON I CAN REMEMBER!

AARGH!

GRRR RWL! KKR RWL!

PLONK!

URF!

TAKE _ZAT_, YOU UNRULY FURBALL!

ZZAP

HOORAY! PIG...I MEAN, LE FOX, SAVED US!

UM.

WAIT, WHO'S IN WHICH BODY NOW?

IT'S ABOUT TIME YOU TWO HAD A **BEAR HUG!**

SCREAM! LE FOX! I KNOW THAT'S YOU!

COME ON PIG, TIME TO GO BACK TO HIBERNATION.

GRRWLL.

HEE HEE!

JAMIE

NEXT TIME - "WOODLAND STORY!"

"WOODLAND STORY!"

PIG GOT HIS HEAD STUCK IN A BEACHBALL!

WE'RE NOT QUITE SURE HOW.

THAT'S DEFINITELY GOING INTO MY BOOK.

OOH, YOU'RE WRITING A BOOK?

CAN IT BE ABOUT DINOSAURS?

SCRIBBLE!

NO. IT'S GOING TO BE A COMPREHENSIVE HISTORY OF THE WOODS! AN ACCOUNT OF ALL THE MAD THINGS THAT HAPPEN, AS WELL AS THE STORY OF WHERE WE ALL CAME FROM!

WELL, THAT'S EASY. I WAS MADE FROM FLOUR, EGGS, ICING SUGAR, SWEETNESS AND CUDDLES!

MY MUMMY SAID SO.

UM, I DON'T THINK SHE MEANT IT LITERALLY, WEENIE.

DID.

I CAME FROM FARRR AWAYYY.

A **GIANT BUTTERFLY** BROUGHT ME TO THE WOODS.

AND IT TOLD ME THAT ONE DAY IT WOULD COME BACK FOR ME!

FLAP! FLAP!

RIIIIIGHT. YOU TWO AREN'T BEING MUCH HELP.

CAN WE STILL BE IN THE BOOK?

CAN I BE A DINOSAUR?

RARR!

PSST! I HEAR YOU ARE WRITING A BOOK ABOUT US.

THAT'S RIGHT, LE FOX. I'M GUESSING YOU WON'T TELL ME ANYTHING THOUGH.

ALL I WILL TELL YOU IS STAY AWAY. STAY AWAY FROM OUR SECRETS. STAY AWAY FROM THE TRUTH. FOR YOU MAY NOT LIKE WHAT YOU FIND.

I AM IN DISGUISE, BY THE WAY.

OKAY, WHATEVER.

THANKS.

STAYYY AWAYYY!

WELL, IIII WAS SENT TO YOUR PLANET BY THE PEOPLE OF EARTH, DESTINED TO BECOME A CONQUEROR OF YOUR WORLD!

MONKYOPIA!

HRGH!

ARE YOU... ARE YOU FALLING ASLEEP IN FRONT OF YOUR GLORIOUS LEADER?

ZZZ.

BANG!

EEE!

THIS IS MY NEWEST INVENTION, THE **BANGBANG**!

IT GOES BANG.

THAT'S ABOUT IT.

AS FOR MY STORY.

I USED TO LIVE IN THE CITY, SCAVENGING FOOD LIKE A COMMON ANIMAL. BUT THEN I DISCOVERED SCIENCE, AND FLEW TO THE WOODS SO I COULD CONTINUE MY RESEARCH IN PEACE!

WOOSH!

WOOOSHH!

OH, THIS IS USELESS! ALL YOUR STORIES ARE RIDICULOUS, NO ONE WILL BELIEVE ANY OF THIS!

RIIIIIP!

RIP!

RIP!

WHAT ABOUT YOU, BUNNY? HOW DID YOU GET HERE?

THAT'S JUST IT...

I DON'T REMEMBER HOW I GOT HERE! I THOUGHT BY WRITING ABOUT YOUR PASTS, I MIGHT REMEMBER MY OWN.

MAYBE IT DOESN'T MATTER WHERE WE COME FROM.

JAMIE

WHAT MATTERS IS WHERE WE ARE NOW.

AND WHERE WE ARE NOW...

...IS MONKEYOPIA!

SIGHH. NOT MONKEY-OPIA.

IS MONKEYOPIA.

BWOO HAR HAR HARRR!

NEXT TIME: "SO MANY MONKEYS!!"

"SO MANY MONKEYS!"

HAHAHA, I'VE DONE IT! I'VE DRIVEN AWAY ALL THE OTHER ANIMALS, AND STRIPPED THE WOODS OF ALL ITS BEAUTY.

THIS FORBIDDING WASTELAND IS NOW MINE! MINE!

IN FACT, I'M SO EXCITED, I'M HAVING A HEART ATTACK.

ERK!

SHRIIIIEK!!

SKUNKY, I HAD A TERRIBLE DREAM LAST NIGHT. IT WAS AWFUL!

DID BANANAS GROW OUT OF YOUR NOSE?

I HAVE THAT DREAM SOMETIMES TOO.

SHUDDER!

WHAT? NO! I DREAMT THAT I FINALLY ACHIEVED MONKEY-O-PIA, THEN DIED BEFORE I COULD ENJOY IT!

I CAN'T DIE!

AHH. MORTALITY.

IT IS THE CYCLE OF LIFE, MONKEY. ALL THINGS IN NATURE GROW, BLOSSOM, THEN WITHER...

NONSENSE! I WANT YOU TO CLONE ME!

CLONE ME! MAKE A SPARE ME, SO WE HAVE A BACK-UP MONKEY.

WE NEED A BACK-UP MONKEY!

61